Orange Cheeks

Jay O'Callahan

Illustrated by
Patricia Raine

PEACHTREE PUBLISHERS, LTD.
Atlanta

I would like to thank Carolee Brockmann for her
editorial assistance in the preparation of this book.
— J.O.

Published by

PEACHTREE PUBLISHERS, LTD.

494 Armour Circle, NE

Atlanta, Georgia 30324

The luminous illustrations were rendered in oils on gessoed board.

Book design and composition: *Candace J. Magee*

Reinforced binding. Manufactured in Mexico.

Printed and bound by Impresora Donneco Internacional S.A. de C.V.

R. R. Donnelley & Sons Co., Division Reynosa/McAllen

1st printing (1993)

Library of Congress Cataloging in Publication Data

O'Callahan, Jay.
    Orange cheeks / Jay O'Callahan ; illustrated by
Patricia Raine.
        p.   cm.
    Summary: When he has a problem while visiting his
grandmother, four-year-old Willie is afraid that he won't
be able to stay overnight again for a year, but his
grandmother helps him make things right.
    ISBN 1-56145-073-1
    [1. Grandmothers—Fiction. 2. Behavior—Fiction.]
I. Raine, Patricia, ill. II. Title.
PZ7.01640r 1993
[E]—dc20
                                 92-43509
                                      CIP
                                      AC

For my son Ted,
whose wide eyes launched a thousand stories

Willie was four and a half. He lived in the country.

The phone rang one day and Willie climbed on the chair and picked up the phone. Willie had a habit of just breathing into the phone.

His grandmother's voice tumbled into his ear. "Hello, Willie."

"How'd you know?"

"I guessed, Willie. Willie, why don't you come over to my house in Cambridge for the night? I know your mom's got a million exams to correct. Would you like to?"

"Yes, grand-*ma-a-a-ah!*"

He handed the phone to his mother, who was unpacking groceries. She was like the wind in a yellow suit, and her voice stretched like elastic.

"Your grandmother wants you to sleep over, Willie," his mother said. "I'm worried you'll get into trouble. Last weekend you cut up all the fruit and put it in the big bowl and poured salt on top."

"By mistake," Willie said.

"I don't want her calling me at ten o'clock tonight because—"

"No trou*bl-l-l-lllle*," Willie said in his deep, up-and-down voice. Willie was helping his mother unpack the groceries. He was being very good.

"I'll tell you this, Willie, late in the day your grandmother can be a bit of a grump."

"No trou*bl-l-l-lllle* ma-*ma-a-a-a*."

"All right, but if there's any trouble you won't go overnight for a year."

Willie had won!

He ran upstairs to his room and got his little bag. He opened his drawer, got six t-shirts and a toothbrush, and ran downstairs.

Willie and his mother drove all the way to Cambridge.

Willie loved Cambridge because all the houses were squeezed together. He looked out the window as they drove around Harvard University, down past the brick fire station, and along Cambridge Street under the wires for the buses. They took a left on Leonard Avenue. His grandmother lived on the second and third floor of number nine.

Willie jumped out of the car onto the brick sidewalk and ran up the wooden front stairs.

The outside stairs were wide

and high. Willie stepped waaaaay up.

He liked the cracks between the boards.

Maybe dimes fell down there.

He hurried so he could press the button before his mother. Willie pushed open the big gray front door and stood in the narrow hall.

Willie saw two doors. Both had a large pane of glass with a curtain so you couldn't see inside. Built into the wall between the doors were two slender slots for mail. The shiny buzzer under the mailbox was waiting for his finger to push it.

Willie pressed it. His fists were clenched and his eyes wide. He didn't breathe. In a second his grandmother would press another button upstairs, and while she held that buzzer, Willie would have to open the door. He'd have to be quick. He didn't want to fail.

Hurry! The buzzer buzzed loud, and Willie's hand grabbed the cold metal door knob and turned it. Willie heard the click. The door opened. He'd done it!

Willie was at the bottom of the dark, narrow stairs. The stairs were filled with the smells of his grandmother's house. The stairs were steep and dark as chocolate.

Willie loved it. He could have spent the whole time right here.

"Come on up, Willie."

"Here I come, grand-*ma-a-a-ah*."

He climbed up to the top and his grandmother leaned down for a hug. He kissed her on her wrinkled, crinkled cheeks. (He loved those cheeks, but he never said anything about them.)

"You'll be in the guest room upstairs," his grandmother said. "There's a prize up there for you."

"Thank you, grand-*ma-a-a-ah*," he said, hurrying up the stairs. His mother's voice caught up with him. "You remember what I said, Willie."

"Don't worry. No trou*bl-l-l-lllle*, ma-*ma-a-a-a*."

His grandmother had done something wonderful. She had pasted silver stars to the ceiling. Willie loved those.

Then Willie saw the prize lying on the table. Two pieces of orange paper, a pair of small scissors, a little jar of paste, and a sharp pencil.

Willie took the scissors, and he cut two circles from the orange paper. Then he put paste on the back of the circles and pressed them to his cheeks. Now he had orange cheeks.

Looking out the window he saw his mother driving away. "Good-bye, ma-*ma-a-a-a,*" he shouted with a victorious grin.

He ran downstairs and his grandmother said just the right thing. "Wonderful cheeks."

"Thank you, grand-*ma-a-a-ah,*" he smiled, jouncing his shoulders.

"We'll have tea in the dining room. But first I'll hang out the wash and you'll go to Mr. Murchison's. You know him."

"The fruit man."

"Yes. He's right next door. He's expecting you. Here are two quarters. Get four pounds of bananas. Yellow ones."

Willie went down the dark, narrow stairs with the wonderful smells out onto the brick sidewalk. There was Mr. Murchison's fruit store.

Its wooden floor was dark and oiled and soft. Willie stepped inside and felt the floor move under his feet. The store smelled good, and the fruit bounced with color. Mr. Murchison was standing there between the oranges and the bananas. He was older than   the bananas. And he was curved like the bananas.

"Hello, Willie," he said in his long, dark voice. "Your grandmother told me you were coming. Nice to see you again." He reached to the top of the banana rack. "I've got four pounds of bananas for you."

Willie shook his head back and forth. "I don't want thoooose."

"Why not?" Mr. Murchison asked.

"They're rotten."

"They're not rotten," mustached Mr. Murchison insisted, laughing. "They're ripe. That's the way you eat bananas."

"Grandma said the yellow ones," Willie said to the floor.

Mr. Murchison replaced the bananas and took yellow ones from the rack. "Someday you'll know better," he rumbled.

"Thank you," Willie said and mumbled, "Think I know better now."

Mr. Murchison seemed to be chewing something distasteful. "I like your cheeks," he finally grunted.

Willie looked up. "I like your cheeks, too."

"Arrrrr."

Willie took the bananas to the back yard, where his grandmother was hanging clothes on the line.

"Good for you, Willie! You're a regular businessman. You go up and play till I finish, and then we'll have tea in the dining room."

Willie entered the back door and stood in the hallway grinning. A secret was coming over him. He was imagining that he *was* a businessman. To him a businessman was someone who took a sharp pencil and made little pencil marks on the walls. Secret ones. But real ones.

Willie almost shook with importance. He made a tiny pencil dot on the hallway wall. He went up to the living room where he made a tiny pencil dot behind the flowered curtains. He pushed the mirror a little to one side and made a businessman's squiggle.

Then Willie decided to make one pencil mark on the dining room wall. No one would ever know. It was important for the business.

He ran into the dining room and saw the dust dancing in the sunlight. The dust was as excited as Willie!

He pushed the chair against the white wall and climbed up. Willie reached way up. He was making a tiny pencil mark when he heard something. Startled, he turned. "Grandma?" No one was there.

Willie turned back to the wall. There was a pencil mark three feet long. Willie's eyes opened almost as wide as his mouth. The pencil mark was huge!

"Ohhhhhhh!"

He tried to erase the pencil mark, but that only made it worse. Then he spat on his hands and tried to wash it off. His hands moved like windshield wipers, but they only made curved black streaks everywhere.

He was in **trouble!**

Willie stared at the mess on the wall. The mess stared back.

"Oh no!" He jumped down and ran into the pantry. "Now I'll have to go home, and I can't come back for a year!"

Willie looked out the window. His grandmother was just about to finish hanging up the wash. He had to do something.

Willie opened the drawer. There was a hammer and two nails.

Willie ran into the dining room. He tore the tablecloth off the table and stood on the chair. He nailed the cloth to the wall.

Now you couldn't see the pencil mark.

Willie ran into the kitchen. His grandmother made the tea and put everything on a tray.

"Come on, Willie, you bring the cookies. We'll have tea in the dining room."

Willie's head seemed to be sinking into his shoulders. "Let's have the tea here."

"We always have tea in here," his grandmother said as she walked into the dining room.

"Willie?" His grandmother sounded bewildered. "The tablecloth's not on the table."

"Willie," she said slowly. She sounded surprised and not happy. "Willie, the dining room cloth is nailed to the wall."

After a silence she heard a tiny voice. "Which wall?"

"You come in and see which wall."

Willie came slowly in. His head sank further into his shoulders. "Oh, that wall," Willie said. "I nailed it to that wall."

Suddenly he began to shake. His whole body trembled and he burst out crying. "Now I can't come back for a year." Willie was crying so hard the tears ran down onto his paper orange cheeks. He began to rub the cheeks, and the paper started shredding.

"Willie!" His grandmother rushed over, kneeling down to hug him. *She* was crying now, and her tears were falling onto his orange cheeks too.

She held him until she could get hold of herself. Then she breathed deeply, saying, "Willie, look at the two of us. This is absurd. It's perfectly all right."

"No it isn't," Willie sobbed. "Now I have to go home. I can't come back for a whole year."

His grandmother stood up, smiling. "Willie, it's fine."

"No it isn't," Willie persisted. "Momma says late in the day you're a grump."

His grandmother's eyes opened wide. Everything, even the dust, stood still. "Hmmm, she does, does she?"

She kept glancing down at him and away. She looked like a bird.

"Well, I'll tell you this, Willie, your mother's no prize either." Willie's mouth dropped open. Clapping her hands together, his grandmother burst out laughing. "But with all her faults I love her still."

They sat down at the table. "Now we'll have tea, and you'll be fine. How many sugars, Willie?"

"Five."

"One," she corrected.

The tea seemed to calm his whole body.

"Now your mother won't know about this," she said with assurance. "It's our secret. You just watch."

His grandmother took the hammer and pulled out the nails. She put the cloth on the table. "I'll sew the nail holes up another time, but we'll fix it so your mother won't know. I'll put a bowl of fruit over one hole and flowers on the other." His grandmother put putty in the holes in the wall. That afternoon she and Willie painted over the pencil mark.

In three hours the paint was dry and the mark was gone. "See," his grandmother beamed. "She won't know."

"She'll know."

"She's my *daughter*. She won't know."

"She's my *mother*. She'll know."

The next morning Willie ran to the living room window about twenty times. "Maybe she can't come today," he said hopefully. Then he saw the car.

"Oh no!" They were going to have tea in the dining room.

When they sat down for tea Willie squirmed. He watched his grandmother pour out the tea. It took forever to fill his cup. He snuck a look at his mother. The tea went on and on.

Finally Willie could be quiet no longer. "Mom! Don't pick the bowl of fruit up!"

"Why would I do that?" His mother stared at the fruit bowl.

"I don't knoooooow." Willie's shoulders curled in delight, and he leaned back grinning.

"What are you looking at?" his mother sighed and looked her knowing look.

"The wall."

"There was trouble, I can tell. What was the trouble?"

Willie sank in his seat. "Tell the trouble, grandma."

"Well, there *was* trouble," his grandmother said, nodding over her tea. "The trouble was Willie and I didn't have enough time together. Is that what you mean, Willie?"

Willie's face shone. "That's what I meeeeeannnn."

A few minutes later they were at the top of the stairs. Willie's grandmother bent over, and Willie kissed her on those wrinkled, crinkled cheeks. (Willie loved those cheeks, but he never said anything about them.)

Then Willie and his mother went down the dark, narrow stairway with the wonderful smells. It was a secret between Willie and his grandmother. The stairs creaked. They knew the secret too.

At the bottom he turned and waved. " 'Bye grand-*ma-a-a-a-ah!*"

" 'Bye Willie."

As they drove away, Willie turned and saw his grandmother waving from her living room window. He couldn't see the dust, but he knew it was dancing there.

When Willie got home he ran up to his room and jumped up and down on his bed. The dust began to dance. Just like at his grandmother's! He wondered if she was still standing at the window.

Willie jumped down and opened his bag. He took out the orange paper and cut two orange circles. He put them in an envelope and whispered into the envelope, "Dear Grandma, here's orange cheeks for you."

About the Author

Jay O'Callahan, described by *Time* magazine as "a genius among storytellers," is in great demand for his storytelling performances. He tours the world, performing at festivals, theaters, museums, and more recently with orchestras. His stories have been heard on National Public Radio, The Voice of America, and "Mr. Roger's Neighborhood." The audio recordings of three of his stories, "Raspberries," "Earth Stories," and "The Island," won Parents' Choice Awards in 1984, 1987, and 1989, respectively. In 1991, he was awarded an NEA grant in the category of Solo Performance/Theater. He lives just south of Cambridge, and Leonard Avenue.

About the Illustrator

Patricia Raine is a versatile artist and illustrator with countless print publications to her credit. A regular illustrator for *The Washington Post* and *U.S. News and World Report* (where she was a weekly political caricaturist), Raine has earned honors from the Society of Illustrators and the Illustrator's Club, as well as from a number of print organizations. She lives near Washington, D.C.